WISE OLD OWL'S CANOE TRIP ADVENTURE

by ROBERT KRAUS

Troll Associates

FOR
PARKER
AND
PAM

The author gratefully acknowledges the background coloring
by Pamela Kraus.

Printed in the United States of America

1   3   5   7   9   10   8   6   4   2

Library of Congress Cataloging-in-Publication Data

Kraus, Robert, (date)
    Wise Old Owl's canoe trip adventure / by Robert Kraus.
        p.   cm.
    Summary: With Slow Turtle as his guide, Wise Old Owl has a
memorable canoe trip over a waterfall.
    ISBN 0-8167-2947-6 (lib. bdg.)   ISBN 0-8167-2948-4 (pbk.)
    [1. Canoes and canoeing—Fiction.   2. Owls—Fiction.   3. Turtles—
Fiction.]   I. Title.
PZ7.K868Wi   1993
[E]—dc20   92-39014

Wise Old Owl sat at his typewriter and could not think of an adventure to write. Am I washed up as a writer? he wondered.

Then he picked up *Forest Fun* magazine and saw an ad.

4

"Just what I need," hooted Wise Old Owl. He dialed the number and, after a very long time, a sleepy voice answered.

"*H-e-l-l-o, S-l-o-w T-u-r-t-l-e.*"

"This is Wise Old Owl, beloved author. I'd like to take your canoe trip."

"You got it," said Slow Turtle, sounding wide awake. "Meet me at the hollow tree at the river bank in ten minutes."

Wise Old Owl hopped into his little red roadster
and tootled through the Magic Forest to the
hollow tree at the river bank.

Slow Turtle recognized Wise Old Owl at once.

"I've read all your books, sir," he said. "It will be an honor to be your guide."

"Thank you," said Wise Old Owl. "It will be an honor to be guided by you."

Slow Turtle looked over Wise Old Owl from head to toe.

"You can't go on a canoe trip in them duds," Slow Turtle said. He gave Wise Old Owl some of his old clothes to put on.

Wise Old Owl ducked behind a bush to change. Soon, he was ready for his canoe trip adventure.

"Now pop on this parachute," said Slow Turtle.

"A parachute on a canoe trip?" said Wise Old Owl.

"You'll see," chuckled Slow Turtle.

Slow Turtle showed Wise Old Owl some basic paddling strokes.

Then, they pushed off! Slow Turtle hopped into the back of the canoe and Wise Old Owl sat at the front.

"Getting there is half the fun!" said Slow Turtle.

"I hope so," said Wise Old Owl.

Slow Turtle and Wise Old Owl paddled through calm waters.

"Enjoy the beautiful scenery while you can," warned Slow Turtle.

"What do you mean?" asked Wise Old Owl.

"You'll see," said Slow Turtle. "You'll see."

Then, the calm waters got choppier and choppier and choppier.

"Now paddle as if your life depends on it, because it does!" Slow Turtle said.

They had not paddled far when the canoe
began to fill with water. Slow Turtle handed
Wise Old Owl a tin can.

"Now bail as if your life depends on it, because
it does!" They managed to stay afloat, but just
barely.

"And now, the highlight of our trip," said Slow Turtle. "We're about to go over the falls. Be sure your parachute is securely fastened."

"GULP!" gulped Wise Old Owl.

CRASHING!
DASHING!
SPLASHING!
Over the falls they went.
SWOOOOOSH!!!

They jumped out of the canoe.

Their parachutes opened. WOOF.

"Boy, do I feel like an endangered species!"
hooted Wise Old Owl.

They floated through the air . . .

... and landed in the river. PLOP.
"Swim for shore," shouted Turtle.
"I can't swim," cried Wise Old Owl.

Thinking fast, he grabbed a floating branch
and kicked his way to shore.

At last, Slow Turtle and Wise Old Owl crawled
out of the river, soaking wet but glad to be alive.

"We've lost our marshmallows," said Slow
Turtle. "We'll have to live off the land."

"But we're only a stone's throw from your
camp," said Wise Old Owl.

"You're so wise," said Slow Turtle.

They started walking.

They had not gone far when who should they meet but Miss Bear, taking her class on a nature walk.

"That's Wise Old Owl," said Pearl Squirrel.

"He's soaking wet," said Chip Chipmunk.

"Who's that turtle with him?" asked Eugene
Fieldmouse.

"What a pleasant surprise," said Wise Old Owl.
"Allow me to introduce my friend and guide,
Slow Turtle."

Slow Turtle built a bonfire. He and Wise Old Owl dried off their wet clothes.

Then everyone toasted marshmallows and sang folk songs, led by Slow Turtle.

"I may be a turtle
But don't laugh, you see
I've a shell on my back
But it is home to me.
Turtle loo ra loo ra
Turtle loo ra loo.
Turtle loo ra loo ra
Turtle loo ra loo."

Soon it was time to go.

"Good-bye, dear Miss Bear and students," said Wise Old Owl. "I have books to write before I sleep."

"And I have songs to sing," said Slow Turtle.

"And I have students to teach," said Miss Bear.

Before long, they were back at the hollow tree by the river bank. Wise Old Owl was happy to change back into his own dry clothes.

"I must be going," said Wise Old Owl. "But first, allow me to say that you are a wonderful guide!"

"Tell your friends to call me at 1-800-T-U-R-T-L-E."

DUCK CROSSING

M.M

"What an adventure," said Wise Old Owl, as he tootled home in his little red roadster. "I'm glad I tried something new. It was just what I needed."

Then, he sat down at his typewriter and wrote WISE OLD OWL'S CANOE TRIP ADVENTURE—the very book you are reading now.